DISCARDED

Love Me, Love You

by Susan Heyboer O'Keefe
Illustrated by Robin Spowart

Boyds Mills Press

Boyds Mills Press, Inc.
A Highlights Company
815 Church Street
Honesdale, Pennsylvania 18431
Printed in China

U.S. Cataloging-in-Publication Data
    (Library of Congress Standards)

O'Keefe, Susan Heyboer.
 Love me, love you / by Susan Heyboer O'Keefe; illustrated by Robin
Spowart. —1st ed.
 [32]p. : col. ill. ; cm.
Summary: A mother rabbit and her baby express their love for
each other throughout the day.
 ISBN 1-56397-837-7
1. Love — Fiction. 2. Rabbits — Fiction. I. Spowart, Robin, ill.
II. Title.
   [E] 21 2001   AC CIP
00-101646

First edition, 2001
The text of this book is set in 28-point Optima.

10 9 8 7 6 5 4 3

Visit our Web site at www.boydsmillspress.com

For Amanda, again
—S. H. O'K.

For Mama Kate
—R. S.

Love me, love my bear.

Love the oatmeal in my hair.

Love me, love my tub.
Bubbles help me splash and scrub.

Love me, love my mess.
Silly ways I like to dress.

Love me, love my teeth.
Two on top and two beneath.

Love me, love you.
Love us both, I do, I do!

Love me, love my ball.

Love my drawing on the wall.

Love me, love my "Boo!"
Love my "Quack," "Meow,"
and "Moo!"

Love me, love my nose.
I can touch it with my toes.

Love me, love my spoon.
Carrot pudding when it's noon.

Love me, love you.
Love us both, I do, I do!

Love me, love my potty.
Big-kid pants all polka-dotty.

Love me, love my book.
Love how grown-up I can look.

Love me, love my thumb.
Tastes so good, I'll give you some.

Love me, love my nap.
I can take it in your lap.

Love me, love you.
Love us all, I do, I do!